WIDE

OPEN

TANZANIA GLOVER

Cover Art by New Levels Graphics

www.tanzaniaglover.com

Booking With Love
332 S Michigan Ave

TANZANIA GLOVER

Suite #121- 2217
Chicago, IL 60604
www.bookingwithlove.com

To my mother. Thanks for reminding me that even though I'm not a gambler, I can never lose when I bet on myself.

SPORT

I must warn you
I am no good
at this game
called...love.
Hand me your heart
and I will fumble it,
as I punt along
my self-doubt
and self-depreciating ways
toward the goal
of overthinking this.
I will return the ball
back to your court
every time
because you are
the point man...
I'll let you call the shots.
and as the shot clock
runs down
so will I....run.
I'm not ready to be

WIDE OPEN

a team player.
Don't pull me off the bench
I'm still healing old injuries.
And my heart is
no longer for
sport.

-Tiffany Richardson

1ˢᵀ QUARTER

"Why do you keep running away from me when you know catching is what I do best? Be here tomorrow or I'm coming to get you."

Without my permission tomorrow had quickly turned into today and after much consideration I'd decided to do the right thing and surrender myself instead of being apprehended. It was probably for the best because I was too cute to be on the lam and thanks to my job my face was too recognizable for a fugitive lifestyle anyway.

My original plan was to continue ignoring him until I could come up with a reasonable repayment schedule, but the thought of Beau Mitchell showing up on my parents' doorstep to collect the pussy he'd paid for had me shaking in my new Chloé boots.

My father would've probably killed us both on principle…that is if he didn't have a heart attack before he could get a good grip on Beau's thick neck. And my mother…well Ma would've certainly acted appalled, but inside I knew she'd be proud that her eldest, her mini me, had gotten a man to pay that much to be with me for one night only. Keeping it all the way real though, I had experienced men twice my size almost seizing on top of me and even *I* didn't think it was worth what he'd paid. But apparently Beau did.

He must've because it wasn't even a full twenty-four hours after he'd won his first and final Super Bowl that my bookie was paid in full and telling me that he wasn't allowed to take bets from me anymore. And considering that I had just been shitting bricks thinking that my dirty little secret would finally be out in the open once I couldn't pay, I didn't exactly oppose the decision.

But I did question who else besides my father would be willing to cough up so much cash to save my neck and my back?

For days while I covered the celebrations and highlights on my first solo show *Touchdown with Tatum Rogers*, I was on pins and needles just waiting for the mystery man to reveal himself. Of course I knew it was a man because I'd been getting the offers since my first job as a sideline reporter with ESPN five years ago.

Players from all the sports I covered and even the ones I didn't offered nonstop to buy me a house, a car, anything my heart desired just to experience the heat between my brown thighs. A few team owners even discretely threw their hats into the ring only to be denied as well because I prided myself on not being able to be bought.

Until now.

And sure even back then the thought of having no bills and worries might have been tempting to the average person, but working in this field taught me that getting caught up with an athlete or anybody athlete adjacent was practically asking for trouble.

Plus with my father being the venerable Coach Rogers for Rutgers University, I never wanted to disappoint him by being one of those girls who were passed around, something that obviously didn't bother my younger sisters. But then again they had never loved the game like I did in the first place.

From birth football was life for me. I was actually far from a tomboy, but I'd been running plays with my father and uncles since I could walk so it ran in my veins. And none of that bullshit touch stuff either. I did full contact and played just as dirty as the son Thomas Rogers had always dreamed of having.

In fact I loved the game so much that I vividly remembered crying like a baby the first time I realized there were no girls in the NFL. I didn't let it stop me though so I played as long as the local teams in Jersey would have me which just so happened to coincide with me getting breasts.

I didn't know who the damn things made more uncomfortable, the coaches or my mother, but neither wanted me on the bottom of a pileup anymore after I got them so I had to quit.

Post football I stayed active by running track and playing tennis all throughout high school, but after starting college I knew I wanted to be reunited with my first love in any way that I could. And since nobody knew the game better than me I decided that not being able to play professionally wouldn't hold me back from leaving my mark on the field. As a woman I knew I would just have to take a different route and do it through sports media.

While I was at Rutgers I interviewed every player that I could, but football was obviously the biggest draw and by my senior year my little blog had gotten an almost cult following. And it certainly didn't hurt that I had my father by my side because I got to see it **all** up close and personal so I always had the scoop.

Sometimes it pained me to have to write about his best players getting into bad situations even before they could potentially make it to the NFL, but it was what I had signed up for as a journalist. It was the stories that I wasn't permitted to write by the university and then later by my network that were even more disturbing though.

Domestic situations were off the charts but of course swept

under the rug and most scandals were several times worse than the stuff that somehow made it to the papers and airwaves. It had even managed to hit a little too close to home at one point early in my postgrad media career.

Most people assumed that the newest tight end for the New York Knights at the time had suddenly decided to leave the team because he got a better offer with the Tampa Bay Gators, but the truth was that Dante Barnes was forced out.

And usually something as "little" as harassing and stalking a woman wouldn't have been worth losing a good player, but with the league already coming off as insensitive to the concerns of women and black folks, and me of course being both, he was out and not allowed to speak to me unless it was game related.

I dreaded the day that I would eventually have to mic up with him again, but luckily my homegirl Karma or maybe even my father had something to do with making sure it'd never happen again. Just days after moving south Dante found himself the victim of an "attempted robbery" gone wrong that led to the disfigurement of both his hands.

It was a strange case that had raised more questions than could be answered, but while his fans mourned what his career could have been I was celebrating. I mean he really thought that he would just be able to skip town and start over making even more money after what he'd done to me, but he never even got to participate in any OTAs in Tampa let alone suit up again. And it was what he deserved.

That was all in my rearview these days though and currently my biggest career issue was the lack of a budget for my on-air wardrobe. I guess they'd assumed because I dressed sporty for my field interviews that they could just throw me in any old thing, but that was not the case.

Even though I considered myself one of if not the best at my current level, even I would admit that a lot of the opportunities I had were due to how I looked. And I mean sure those first few exclusives at Rutgers were because every player wanted to be nice to the coach's kid, but being pretty certainly didn't hurt things either.

Complaining to the network about the issue was useless though because their solution was pointing out that this sort of thing should've been put in my contract and ultimately they were right. But my bum agent dropping the ball aside, renegotiations wouldn't come around again until the following season and I refused to look like a weather girl until then.

I had no choice but to charge the expenses to the game and then to my credit cards.

It started off small, a few midrange dresses for the first batch of episodes, but as my *TDTR* ratings grew so did the price tag on just about everything that touched my body. My shoes spoke Italian and the bundles that gave me my sleek, professional bob cost just as much because God was forgiving, but the cameras weren't.

Before long my debt was looking like somebody's student loans and I didn't even know how to begin climbing out of the hole because budgeting was not exactly in my vocabulary in the first place. And when I wasn't working I was traveling or in the city running up a tab with my friends so that left no time to be responsible hence me recently moving back home to Jersey from Manhattan to save money.

Being home wasn't as bad as it sounded though because everybody loved having me close by again and for the most part my parents treated me like an adult. I was hardly there anyway, but I enjoyed coming home late to fresh folded laundry and leftovers because my mother believed in cooking seven days a week. My folks had no problem feeding me and continuing to put a roof over my head, but I'd abused their wallets so much that they were closed until further notice.

It was a shame too because in the past when I'd found myself having money problems, I had just asked my father for a bailout and he always came through for me because he had it like that. But this time was a little different because my debt was beyond a lecture on spending habits and creeping into staging an intervention for a shopping addiction territory.

So yep trying to live like Carrie Bradshaw had me even further in the broke house while I was supposed to be saving on rent and bills and the only way I knew how to come up with some quick cash was making bets.

Again nobody knew the game or the players like I did so at first it was like taking candy from a baby and I was able to pay off all of my bills and then some. But it didn't take long for me to get greedy and lose it all in one fell swoop.

I'd bet all I had and even a little I didn't on the Super Bowl because everybody knew there was no way in hell that the Knights would pull off a win against the Chicago Cougars. Luck had been on their side all season long as they won games that nobody saw them even coming close to winning, but most analysts were sure that it would run out come Super Bowl Sunday.

Somehow every single prediction including my own was wrong though and The New York Knights, who hadn't won a Super Bowl since before I was born, were now the world champions and I was fucked. Outside of athletes nobody I knew had that kind of money lying around and I certainly wouldn't have it for at least another lifetime so I knew it was only a matter of time before I got exposed by my bookie to recoup something.

And after that happened I knew I would surely be fired from the network because even though sports betting had become legal a while ago, per our contracts we still weren't allowed to partake. But before any of that got the chance to get set into motion, my debt was cleared and I finally got the phone call I'd been waiting for.

"I'm disappointed in you, Rogers," Beau's gruff voice said in a teasing, sing-song manner. "I really thought you were just as strait-laced as your old man, but you had me fooled good."

"Wait it was you?" It was humanly impossible to be more annoyed than I was from hearing him on my line so I didn't even try to fake it. "What the hell do you want now?"

"Not over the phone. When can I see you?"

"Tonight if you turn on your TV."

"I'm not playing. When are you free?"

"For you Beau? Never." I could hear his smile from my end, but it did nothing to help my frown.

"We're gonna have to fix that then, huh?"

I would never tell him or anybody else, but I still remembered the feeling of relief that came over me when the call ended that day a couple weeks ago. I was repulsed by the idea of having to do something strange for a little change with anybody, but I was glad that it was somebody I was at least familiar with and maybe even attracted to on some level.

Alright look whatever. For the record nobody disliked Beau

"The Blizzard" Mitchell more than me, but even I couldn't pretend like the man wasn't fine as fine could be. That wasn't even up for debate. But I still couldn't stand his fine, cocky, overrated ass and now that he'd actually won a championship I knew I would barely be able to fit in a room with him and his new even bigger head.

Men like him were the reason I had my rules against dating athletes in the first place. And despite being flirtatious and asking me out every chance he got, he never missed the opportunity to challenge me in ways that he never did with male journalists. Stephen A. Smith could say whatever he wanted about Beau and his butter fingers or incomplete passes, but let me say the same thing and I got nothing but lip from him.

"I don't want you out here slacking just because you're a woman and you're bad, Rogers. If you're gonna do this then be the best at it," he'd told me after being traded back to the Knights two years ago.

"Maybe take your own advice then and get a ring already before it's too late."

"Bet. And after I get my ring, I'm coming for you next."

2ND QUARTER

I never skipped breakfast. Ever. My whole life both my mother and father stressed that it was the most important meal of the day so no matter how late I was running I always made time to get something filling to keep me fueled up for my day.

Well today I skipped breakfast. And it had nothing to do with a lack of hunger since my stomach instantly growled at the smell of my mother's homemade buttermilk biscuits. But I was just too nervous to eat anything after reading a text message from Beau about an hour ago.

"A helicopter? Why are you like this?"

"I've waited long enough for this. Ain't nobody got time for you to drive all the way here."

I was already anxious enough every time I boarded a plane, but there was just something about helicopters that didn't sit right with my spirit so this day was already off to a rough start.

I tried not to focus on it too much though and instead got

dressed for the brick February weather outside. If this had been an actual date more effort would've been put in, but since my clothes probably wouldn't be on for very long I settled for a comfortable red flannel shirt and a pair of thick, cozy leggings.

My hair didn't bounce about as much as it did when it was freshly done the other week, but I definitely wasn't getting it touched up just to mess it up…if he could mess it up.

I'd heard all the stories about how a lot of players left all they had on the field and barely had any stamina in the bedroom. And not that I was looking forward to this or anything, but if I had to do it I didn't want to hate it either.

Beau had been trying to meet in the city for the last couple weeks, but since I didn't want anybody I knew to see me with him I finally just told him that I would come to his new house out in Connecticut. The last time I'd interviewed him it'd been at his apartment over in Lenox Hill, but a while ago I'd heard through the grapevine that he was finally ready to do the homeowner thing.

I thought it was a little late in his career to be buying extravagant houses, but clearly he had some money lying around to be able to come through for me on such short notice.

It had been over a decade since I'd last had to sneak out of the house, but since today was D-Day in more ways than one, a girl had to do what a girl had to do. It wasn't like I would have to explain where I was going or anything, but I just didn't want to see anybody and feel any guiltier than I already did.

Aside from saying grace and praying before games, we weren't exactly the most religious family, but I knew my actions as of late would be frowned upon if anybody ever found out so I covered my tracks as best as I could. I carefully tip-toed passed my mother and sister washing dishes in the kitchen then slowly slipped into my boots by the front door, but when I went to put on my coat I was accosted by the devil herself.

"You literally see it's me, Lucy. Shut up!" I barked back at my mother's little ugly Pomeranian. I had been back home for six months now and she still treated me like I was company since she had free reign over my room until now.

That was all the noise it took to jolt my father from his after breakfast coma on the couch. As he yawned loudly then stretched I had to admit that my old man still looked good for his age except for that growing tire around his waist that we had all been teasing him about lately.

"Where you sneaking off to, Peanut?" he asked groggily as he sat up to give me his full attention. I stammered for a second before the question was answered from behind him.

"To Beau Mitchell's house," my youngest sister Tara said with a sneaky twinkle in her eye so I knew she must've been listening to my conversations again.

I was still surprised her nosy behind didn't know my biggest secret just yet, but that was why I had gone paperless for all my bills. My mother already refused to stop opening my junk mail so I knew nobody would respect anything else unless their lives depended on it.

"Hasn't he had enough press already?" my father asked automatically assuming that it had to be work related since he knew how much I despised Beau.

"Well yeah, but we're going in a different direction with this story," I said quickly then turned my attention to my mother before anybody realized I was lying.

"Baby you leaving? I wanted you to help me with the lasagna," she said as she pointed to the ingredients she'd began sitting out on the counter.

They had literally just finished cleaning up from breakfast and they were already about to start prepping for dinner because lasagna was an all-day affair in this household. You would have thought my mother was somebody's Sicilian Nonna the way she insisted on making everything even the noodles from scratch.

"I can't. Make Daddy help you for once since you know he's gonna eat half of it," I teased as I messed with the salt and pepper hair on his head. It was a known fact that he was only affable to us because with everybody else he could go from teddy bear to tiger faster than a center could snap the ball.

"Alright well be careful. Dinner's at seven and I want you here with us for a change, you hear me?" she asked me with a hand on her hip.

Sunday dinners meant everything to her because it was the only day that we were all usually guaranteed to be home at the same time to enjoy her homecooked meals. And you wouldn't know it by looking at her, but just because she didn't resemble anybody's Big Mama didn't mean that she couldn't throw down.

"I know. I'll try to be back by then, but I can't really say how long this thing is gonna take." Before she could start in about that being my go-to excuse I cut her off. "Next Sunday I promise I'll be here all day and I'll pick every bunch of greens you put in front of me with a smile on my face."

I playfully pushed Tara out of the way to kiss my mother's round cheek, but before I could wrap up the mushy moment the doorbell was ringing and Lucy was barking again.

"Who could that possibly be this early?" she asked no one in particular.

Naturally as the protector of the family, my father rose from his seat and prepared to defend us from the likes of an Amazon delivery driver or possibly a Jehovah's Witness. Of course it had absolutely nothing to do with him being just as nosy as he often accused all women of being.

I literally almost gasped when the door was opened wide enough to reveal Beau standing there. I could've fainted when he was invited in from the cold, but that would've blown my entire cover so I tried to act as normal as possible.

Beau's smile reached his eyes when he saw my initial reaction, but first he addressed my mother then my father out of respect.

"Sorry to bother you at home, Coach. I just wanted to personally make sure Tatum got to Connecticut safely. I know she had some trouble the last couple times she was supposed to come," he said evenly before turning to look down at me.

He was currently the tallest wide receiver in the league at six-seven so he stood a full foot taller than me when I wasn't wearing heels.

"Aw isn't that sweet. You're a good man, Beau," my mother said before my father decided to be phony and congratulate him on his recent win.

He had done nothing but criticize Beau's career since he'd petitioned to join the draft early against his advice years ago, but I guess seeing how he'd performed with the Knights the last couple seasons was enough to humble us all.

I stood there alone for a while just awkwardly waiting for their conversation to end because my mother and Tara dipped out whenever sports were mentioned.

"Alright don't be too hard on him, Peanut," my father said before reaching for the Sunday paper which meant he was about to blow up the bathroom soon.

When it was just us in the family room I walked over then gestured for Beau to bend down so I could whisper in his ear since I knew Tara's big ears could still be listening in.

"Why did you come here? I was on my way," I said before letting him see that I had all my things and was already heading out.

"You've said that twice already and I wasn't taking any chances today. Now c'mon

Peanut," he teased me with a wide grin as he nodded towards the door. "Our ride is waiting."

"Yeah so about that…I'm just gonna drive. I'll probably get there around noonish so still pretty early with enough time for whatever torture you have planned for me."

"Spending time with me is torture now?"

"The cruel and unusual kind actually."

"We'll see if you change your mind about that by tonight, but in the meantime get your ass in the car because you're getting on that helicopter," he said like he and not the man currently lighting up the downstairs bathroom was my father.

"Says who?" I asked defiantly with my arms folded over my chest because as long as I got there, it shouldn't have mattered how.

He looked around for a second to make sure that nobody but Lucy was watching us before backing me into the mantle. The fireplace hadn't been lit for a few days, but I swore I felt the temperature rise with him so close to me.

"Says me." Authority laced his tone before he leaned in so that our eyes could almost meet. "Unless you want me to go ask

Coach what he thinks about all of this?"

3ᴿᴰ QUARTER

So the helicopter ride actually wasn't even that bad. I prayed and closed my eyes for most of it and Beau let me hold onto him when we took off then again when we landed. It was on the smaller side so he was almost too big for his seat, but I didn't complain because having him to squeeze made me feel a little bit safer.

I tried to ignore the way his cologne lingered on me because he smelled like rich, cocky nigga in the best way possible and that was something I'd always appreciated about him. Back when I still did locker room interviews I had encountered some of the funkiest funk known to man and that along with "accidentally" being flashed was enough reason for me to wait outside for a quote.

My friends assumed that getting to talk to fine, paid and sweaty men would be a job perk, but the novelty quickly wore off once I got a whiff of them after a game. Some didn't shower for days for good luck effectively making the place smell like death, but Beau always stood out in that regard because his scent could only be described as sweaty delight. And even though he didn't overdo it, in general I could tell he took pride in his appearance because he always looked well put together.

Even now in just a dark hoodie and jeans, he looked good enough to eat, but just thinking about eating had my stomach rumbling. And I guess it'd turned out to be a good thing that I hadn't eaten breakfast because I probably would've lost it in the air. But as we were stepping down from the loud hunk of flying metal, I made him promise to feed me as soon as possible before I got hangry.

"See that wasn't so bad, was it?" he asked after he'd helped me into his waiting car.

"No, but I prefer Steph Curry's helicopter because it's bigger. His whole family can fit."

"That's 'cause Steph's contract is bigger too. And did you give him a hard time like you did with me?"

"I sure did not. It was after Game Six and there was no way I was missing out on my interview."

"Nah everybody knows you like the NBA niggas better than us anyway."

"I do not. I think I have more fun with them, but that's because I'm more invested in football. With basketball I can just relax and enjoy the game."

"Either that or you know you're gonna end up with a hooper," he accused as he took his eyes off the road for a second to look over at me.

"You know the rules Beau. If his profession involves a score, he'll definitely be a whore," I told him honestly even though I hadn't always believed that to be true.

You couldn't tell young Tatum that I wouldn't be happily married to a football player by now, but that was before I grew up and realized they weren't the heroes that everybody believed them to be. They were just men like any other only their egos couldn't be deflated like footballs.

Even my father had his own missteps back in the day. I didn't like it or think it was fair, but I minded my black ass business because my mother seemed happy now. And knowing her she had probably done some dirt of her own too because she was just as vindictive as I could be.

Beau didn't even try to argue against my point about male athletes being hypersexual and instead tried to change the subject to something lighter. I wouldn't let him though. Just because I was here for pleasure and not business didn't mean that I wouldn't ask the one question I knew he'd been lying about in his recent interviews.

"Since you know my biggest secret, I think it's only fair that you tell me yours. Why are you *really* retiring so early?"

I mean sure his speed had slightly declined with age, but his body control and footwork could have easily gotten him through another contract and a few more seasons so I knew the cause was likely something internal.

"Aren't you tired of hearing the same answer? I wanted to go out on top and I did. End of story." He said it in a way that almost begged me to pry for more because he didn't even try to sound convincing.

"Off the record," I assured him even though the phrase was like kryptonite to me. He glanced over once more before putting both hands on the wheel.

"After I got traded here again I ran into T.O. and I asked him when he knew it was time to retire. You know what he told me?" he asked and I couldn't help but immediately regret saying this wouldn't be on the record. "He said for some guys unfortunately their bodies let them know, but the lucky ones' minds let them know."

"So your mind let you know then?"

"I don't know. I guess I just used to dream about the game more, but the last couple years other stuff has been taking its place."

"Stuff like what?" I asked simply because no matter how much thought I put into a question, I never could get him to open up to me like other guys did.

Outside of his stats I just knew he grew up in a rough neighborhood in Camden, but it was never something he was willing to engage about.

"Rogers, the last thing I want to do with you today is talk about football," he said through a yawn and that made me want to know the first thing that he *did* want to do with me.

"Okay, but just one more question then. Nobody's here so can you finally just admit what you know about Deflategate?"

Like the rest of the world I'd heard every bullshit theory, but I knew Beau knew the real story since his best friend Renny James had played for New England that season.

"Off the record?" he asked with a grin.

"Of course."

"No. Say the words again," he demanded like he knew I was on bullshit this time and I laughed because I was.

"Okay fine. *Off the record* for real then."

"Alright Ren said he ain't have anything to do with it, but yeah Brady did that shit and Belichick orchestrated it. I still don't know how they covered it all up because a nigga like me would've told the minute I got pressed," he said seriously but then immediately started laughing at the situation.

"Stop lying. You know Don Dada Belichick said it's *blood in, blood out*. That's how snitches get stitches."

"Nah when you got money you just get immunity and a story to tell your friends. You know that," he said with a wink that suddenly made me remember what I was actually here for.

"Hey speaking of keeping things off the record, you're not gonna make this a story for your friends, are you?" I was already looking at his side profile so I saw his jaw clench before he stopped at a red light then made seemingly sincere eye contact with me.

"Everything that happens today goes right in the vault. I would never hear the end of it if Ren found out how much I spent on you," he chuckled out.

"Beau, I'm serious. You know I can't have this getting back to my father or the network or anybody. Promise me you'll keep it between us."

"Relax. You know I got you, Rogers," he said trying to reassure me, but that didn't stop my heavy sigh as he made a turn into an elite looking residential neighborhood. "What's that about?"

"Nothing, but look we both know why I'm here. Let's just get this out of the way so I can get back home and you can get back to whatever you do in the off-season. I don't care what kind of freaky shit you're into, but I'm not doing it. We're not putting anything up my butt and I'm not going anywhere near yours so please don't ask," I said with as much confidence as possible since I didn't want him to think my body was just a free for all because of what he'd spent.

"Yo what the hell are you talking about?" he asked with confused brows as he suddenly stopped the car in front of two heavy iron gates. I could briefly see that the estate behind them was beautiful, but I couldn't keep my eyes on it with him verbally demanding my attention again.

"Wait you think I'm trying to buy you with this?" he asked like the thought was completely absurd. "I did this out of respect for Coach. I'm not expecting anything from you."

"I call bullshit. All of that cryptic 'Don't make me come and get you' shit you said was about me paying you back in coochie not cash," I accused, but he continued to completely dismiss the notion.

"Rogers, I've been had bread and I've been wanting you. If I thought you could be bought, trust me this would've happened two contracts ago," he said lightheartedly before a mischievous realization came to mind. "Yo this is wild though. You really came here to fuck me. I didn't know you spoke Bird so fluently."

"Fuck you. I wasn't actually gonna do it, stupid. I just wanted to see if you were really as bad as I thought you were."

"Hold up. Why am I the bad guy here? What have I ever done to you?"

"Um…you've only been making my job harder than it has to be for no reason for years."

"Why because I don't let you get away with parroting what these other niggas say?"

"First of all I don't have to parrot anything. I know my shit. If anything you've seen them stealing my hot takes and getting praised for it so don't even try that with me, Beau," I said matter-of-factly because my biggest pet peeve was people assuming I was some airhead who just got by on being cute.

"Yeah I've seen that, but more than that I've seen you holding back and not saying shit until somebody else said it first because you were scared. Where you're at is cool for now, but I know for a fact you're never getting to the next level if you're still scared."

"Thanks for the advice. I'll take it into consideration," I said sarcastically as he reached outside his window to finally press the button to open the gates that led to his long curved driveway.

I was surprised to see that there wasn't a luxury car for every day of the week parked out front like there were at some of the players' houses I had been to.

"Oh so you can commentate on the mistakes that I make on the field, but I can't tell you when I see you playing scared on air too?"

"I'm not scared of anything except for losing my show."

"Nah. I'm hip to you now. You act all serious and you got your little Taraji bob over there, but you're nothing like how you act when the cameras are around. In fact you're a hypocrite."

"How am I a hypocrite?" I asked incredulously because now he was just saying shit to get a rise out of me.

"How are you not? You talk cash shit about niggas

mismanaging money and going broke after retirement when you're doing the same shit."

"Me betting on the Super Bowl and losing is not the same thing as over eighty percent of y'all going broke after three years out of the league," I said trying to downplay how much I lost before swinging things back to the original topic.

"And if you're to be believed and today really isn't about sex then why am I here? You could've just jumped in my Twitter comments like you always do when you feel like annoying me."

"Nah this was something that had to be done in person. You

were loud and wrong all season long about me so now *I* get the last laugh. Ha ha ha," he said obnoxiously as he got out of the car. I didn't wait for him to come around to my side before I was up and on my feet too.

"Well congrats. You got it. So am I free to go now because I will gladly find my own way home if it means getting away from you."

"Chill. First I got some stuff for us to get into then we're going to dinner."

"But I already told you I'm not going out in public with you."

"Yeah I know. That's why we're doing everything here."

"Wait what do you mean by everything?" I asked curiously before I realized what was actually going on here. It didn't have anything to do with looking out for my father or rubbing his win in my face. This was him finally *coming for me* like he said he would do years ago.

"Beau, please tell me that all of this is not your sick, sad way of trying to take me on a date. Please," I begged him because my mind could not take any more plot twists today.

"Would you have accepted my invitation if I was straightforward?" he asked rhetorically, not even trying to deny it anymore. "A'ight then come on before I get *Daddy Dearest* on the phone," he teased me again knowing that just mentioning my father would make me act right.

"This is literally blackmail and lowkey kidnapping too. I might could even get you arrested. I know the cops around here would love to handcuff your black ass," I said looking around the foyer as he led us inside.

He was obviously still moving in so it was mostly empty, but the high ceilings and twin winding staircases were really nice as is.

"Probably but you ain't gonna call them since you want to be here." He took off his boots by the door so I followed his lead and got comfortable too.

"Right and me dodging you for the last couple weeks was just an act."

"Funny you should say that because I'm starting to think it was. You claim you wouldn't have slept with me, but I'm not buying it. If it were true then you would've at least offered to pay me back," he said thinking he was about to trip me up.

"Well obviously I can't afford to right now, genius."

"Nah you make decent bread. It might've taken a few years, but see here's what I think. You didn't make it an option because you didn't want it to be one. You would've let it happen so you'd have an excuse to do something that you've been wanting to do anyway."

"You're really crazy, you know that? You have to be to somehow turn you sticking your nose and your wallet in my business into me wanting to sleep with you."

"If I'm wrong then why are you here Tatum?" I hesitated for a second not because I was unsure, but because he usually only used my first name in mixed company.

"Is this *Finding Dory* or something? I'm here because you literally just came to my house and threatened to tell my father everything."

"C'mon. You knew I wouldn't," he said playfully, but it actually just angered me. I'd just barely gotten my sock clad feet out of my snow boots and I was already bending over to put them back on.

I had pointlessly worked myself up for weeks over this situation when it was just him playing mind games with me. And a tiny, I mean miniscule, part of me was also upset that I had gone through the hassle of shaving everything, I mean **everything**, anticipating finally ending the sex drought I'd been in since moving back home.

"I know you're not leaving?" he asked like he didn't see me in front of him doing bunny ears with my shoelaces.

"Yeah I am. I'll just have my father write you a check. I would rather him be disappointed in me than have to participate in this weirdo shit you concocted here today."

"So that's it? You're really just gonna leave without even

thanking me?" he asked after I'd stood upright again.

"Thank you for what exactly? I never even asked for your help."

"Yeah but your ungrateful ass still got it. Do you know what that man would've done to you if you didn't come up with his money?" he questioned, raising his voice and sounding genuinely concerned.

"I could've handled it myself, Beau," I said dismissively because I honestly hadn't thought about that part since I was too worried about losing my job and my dignity.

He just glared at me for a second before shaking his head and walking towards the stairs.

"Fuck it then. Lock the door on your way out." He sounded calm, but his body language was anything but as his heavy feet almost stomped upstairs.

I knew I should've just done like he'd said and let myself out, but instead I followed after him wanting to make sure I pissed him off even more before I left.

"Oh you're mad now?" I asked his back because he continued walking down a long hallway even after seeing that I was right behind him.

"You're fucking right I'm mad. Because instead of going out and celebrating something I've been working for my whole life, I was busy looking out for your spoiled ass that night like I've always done."

"Negro please. When have you ever had to look out for me?" He stopped so suddenly that I almost walked into him.

"Off the record?" he asked smugly.

"Off the fucking record," I said because I couldn't wait to hear this tall tale.

He slowly turned back around, but instead of keeping the space that was already between us, he took a step and then another until my nose was in his chest. Both of his hands rested on the wall behind my head as he peered down at me and pressed his body into mine.

"Nobody, not even Coach has had the guts to do the shit that I've done for you," he said vaguely before continuing. "He only got that nigga traded. Meanwhile I made sure that he would never lay another finger on you or anybody else."

From his stance I could tell that he was proud of what he was saying and for some reason his words sent a heated chill up my spine. I inhaled a big breath trying to think clearly before I acted impulsively, but it just made for more contact between him and my breasts.

"Beau, are you talking about Dante?" I asked just to be sure I wasn't hearing things.

"You know exactly what I'm talking about, Tatum. He touched you so his hands had to pay the price. And the only reason I let him live was so he could suffer while having to continue to see you win."

The way he talked so casually about potentially ending a man's life should've made me scared since I was now trapped underneath his body. But I was far from afraid because I knew the only pain he would subject me to would be accompanied by a whole lot of pleasure.

The journalistic part of me had a million questions. I wanted to know the whens, the wheres and the whys. But all of that would have to wait a bit longer because for now the primal, animalistic part of me wanted to finally give him a proper thank you.

4TH QUARTER

My hands were pinned above my head just how I liked and I was getting wetter by the second, but unfortunately Beau and I had now traded places. Now he was the one with the attitude and playing hard to get, while I was just trying to convince him to put his Twitter fingers to better use.

Finding out what he'd done, risking his freedom and career to avenge me, had turned me on so fast that I could've been mistaken for a light switch. I wanted him. And I would have him.

It was freeing to finally admit it because every time he'd made a move on me in the past I had done a good job convincing myself that I was making the right decision by denying him.

I had been tempted by a few different players over the years but none more so than Beau. There was just something about the way he looked at me with those deep, dangerous brown eyes that let me know I would be in for one hell of a ride if I ever let him in.

And now after all of his grandstanding, he was getting his payback by making *me* beg for it. There was no way I could've seen this role reversal coming, but I was about to play him better than he ever could since I wasn't leaving until I scored.

"C'mon Beau. I said I was sorry. Now this is your two-minute warning before you gotta let me make it all up to you," I said as I let my hard nipples graze him.

"Yo you must really think highly of yourself. First you thought you could use your pussy as currency and now you're acting like finally giving it to me is gonna make me not be mad at you anymore."

"What can I say? I have all-purpose pussy. You should have some," I joked which just made him smile down at me then lie through his teeth.

"I don't want it anymore. And I already told you no means no so you need to turn that little tight end around and go home, Rogers," he teased me with his lips dangerously hovering above mine.

His mouth said *no*, but his body was saying **I'm about to tackle you** as his growing erection pressed into my bellybutton. Still I decided to let him believe that he was angry enough to actually resist me.

"Okay. Let me go then," I dared him, but he kept me pinned to the wall a little longer.

"If I let you go, do you promise to keep your hands to yourself this time?" he asked in a fake stern voice so I nodded my head. "Alright now you be a good girl and get home before I change my mind and give you something you ain't used to."

He slowly loosened the grip he had on my wrists then stepped backwards until his back reached the opposite wall. He couldn't take his eyes off of me if he wanted to so after clearing my throat and regaining my composure, I walked back towards the stairs and gave him something to really admire.

My red flannel shirt hit the floor first.

A few feet later I kicked off my boots again.

I'd planned on leaving a trail of clothes leading down the stairs so that he could fuck me hard while I held on to the railing. But by the time I got over to the top of the stairs and coyly bent at the waist to slide both my panties and leggings down, he was already on his knees behind me with his tongue swiping right.

I was caught off guard because I was used to taking sex slowly and working up to this point. I loved to kiss and get well-acquainted with a man's body before just diving right in. But none of that stopped me from poking it out more and giving him even better access to my clit.

"Mm Beau, you're the first man who's ever kissed those lips before the ones on my face," I moaned out at the way he was already greedily slurping me up.

"I got you. I'mma let you taste it in a minute," he assured me between licks, but the way he got settled on the floor said otherwise.

Standing in nothing but my thick, winter socks I was devoured every which way until my legs nearly gave out. If it wasn't for the railing in front of me I would've probably fallen to my death, but instead I was currently living the best possible life that could be lived.

"Beau, please stop! Shit!" I whined as my legs finally buckled underneath me.

All of a sudden I fell backwards into his lap and felt warm, hard dick waiting on me to get my shit together. I thought I'd heard him unzipping his jeans and giving himself some of the same feelings that he had been giving me, but I couldn't be too sure because just a few minutes ago he had made me come so hard my damn ears popped like I was on a plane.

He used his shirt to wipe away the juices that were dripping down his face then removed it completely.

"Ay stand up real quick," he ordered calmly, but I couldn't move an inch with my wobbly legs and still trembling body so I just slid off of him.

He stood to his feet then watched me from above as he finished undressing. And despite how downright fuckable he looked, I still felt a pang in my chest when I noticed his hands were shaking as he undid his pants.

"You nervous or something?" I asked playfully and of course he denied it at first.

"A'ight a little bit," he admitted with a smirk before I helped him pull his jeans over his muscular ankles. That's when I saw that he was uncut, but I didn't mind at all because he smelled clean and masculine.

"You still hungry, right?" he asked with a smirk as he stroked himself in front of my face.

I nodded because I didn't even too much care about real food anymore since now my pussy's meat cravings were more important.

I sat up on the heels of my feet then wet my lips to prepare my mouth for him.

"Open wider," he instructed as he pushed his thick, bulbous head in between my lips, but it was easier said than done because my mouth was already almost full of him.

He flexed it in my hand when I took hold of it to lick the tip and get it as wet as possible before trying to put his baby anaconda in again.

"You know I never noticed it before, but you talk a lot of shit to have such a little ass mouth, Rogers."

"You think so?" I asked as I slapped it against my tongue a few times then licked the underside. "Wait you don't think it's too big to fit everywhere, do you?" I asked innocently before sucking and slobbering on each of his balls.

That was the wrong thing to do because it looked like The Blizzard was about to melt right where he stood.

"Fuck. C'mon. There's only one way to find out," he said before suddenly lifting me up by my shoulders.

I was more than okay to move on my own now, but he grabbed me by the waist and made me wrap my legs around him. The head wasn't all the way in yet, but I purposely pushed down on it a little so that I could grip the tip.

"Fuck. I think I'mma need a cigarette after this shit," he said before wiping his forehead.

"Ew I didn't know you smoked."

"I don't," he let me know then we both exploded with laughter. I didn't know why it was so funny, but it just was and he nearly dropped me before using the wall to hold me up.

After that he raised me higher so that I could reach his lips and for a second I forgot about everything around us. Even though we'd both just had these same mouths where the sun didn't shine, there was still an innocence in the air as we leaned in to let our lips get acquainted for the first time. And him moaning in my mouth was all it took to get my core back pulsing.

"Hey is there a bed in this place because I think we've already shown out enough in this hallway?" He grinned before pecking my lips once more.

"Yeah. We can go down to my room."

He hoisted me up and secured my legs around his waist before taking calculated steps to the master bedroom. We still bumped around a little though because we refused to stop kissing and sucking on each other's lips.

"This is not your room. This is bigger than my last apartment," I marveled as I looked around and spotted the biggest, longest bed I had ever seen in my life.

It seemed to go on for miles and I imagined us rolling around every inch until our bodies made us stop. He playfully tossed me on the bed and I bounced higher than I expected to.

Instinctively I laughed out loud, but playtime was clearly over as he climbed in after me then met me in the center. My legs were already open so he just got comfortable between them again.

He almost looked possessed before groaning and telling me that he could suck on my pussy forever and never get tired of it. I came right then again and felt like I couldn't take anything else right as he started exploring me with his fingers. My thighs instantly acted like pliers and squeezed his head as he stared in my eyes.

"Mm. Can you please just fuck me already?" I complained

with an arched back because his fingers were long enough to touch my soul and they had me twisting around in sweet agony.

I didn't have to ask twice because he suddenly withdrew them then stood upright before dragging me by my legs to one of the bed's four corners. My feet were pointed to the ceiling as he finally lined his body up to enter me.

I didn't think anything of it when he removed the socks from my feet, but when he stuck his long, warm tongue between my toes then sucked them one by one I knew I was officially not dealing with a regular man anymore.

Beau was doing some shit that would have the Jersey girl in me ready to fight any broad who tried to get in on this action too.

All thoughts of violence instantly ceased though when he finally pushed what felt like a damn tree trunk inside of me. I prided myself on never running from dick because I always made sure I was wet enough to take on any serpent, but this was different.

"Oh my God. I can't do this," I said tapping out after a minute of him trying to get me adjusted to him.

"You want to stop?" he asked, but I just shook my head and

asked him to rub my clit. He did that and sucked my toes again which helped, but I felt like the angle we were at was the real issue. Like he was reading my mind he said, "Get on top. I don't want to hurt you."

We quickly switched places and as I sat up on my knees I was almost mesmerized at the way his dick arrogantly swayed then stood upright with no assistance. I usually preferred a nice curve, but his got me excited enough to do my best Fonzie impersonation and *sit on it*.

This was much better. I put both hands on his neck as I rocked back and forth trying to take a little more than the tip each time.

I was already exhausted, but I rode him hard until it was a struggle to catch my breath. He just laid there enjoying my breasts in his face because he finally got to latch onto them. I knew he was getting ready to finish when he couldn't suck on them anymore and just threw his head back and looked at the ceiling.

"Oh shit. Tatum," he groaned loudly as he began throwing his dick upwards at me to catch his nut.

There was so much heat and wetness between us now that

over half of him was effortlessly entering me and hitting the spot that would ultimately make me convulse. My orgasm came out of nowhere like a tick and my body jerked all about trying to run away from how good it felt, but that was an impossible task.

Right when I was starting to calm down, Beau gripped my hips tightly then forced as much as he could into me while he spilled all he had. He twitched and moaned in a way that I hadn't heard him do yet and I knew he was officially spent too.

I collapsed into his chest and tried to coach him through breathing like we were at a

Lamaze class. I had been watching him play ball since his college years and I had never seen him look so tired before. I smiled at the thought because I knew I had definitely given him his money's worth in one round.

"What are you thinking about?" he asked breathlessly trying to take the attention off of how I had just worked him over.

"Food and lots of it. I'm really hungry now," I told him because now that I was coming down from clouds seven, eight, *and* nine I could focus on my stomach growling between us.

"Even after all that dick I just fed you?" he chuckled out.

"See this is why it took so long for me to let you feed me anything. And what happened to this great, romantic first date you had planned? I assume it came with a meal."

"Oh we're canceling all that shit. You're mine now so I'm not letting you hide me in the house. We're about to take this shit on the road," he said playfully even though I could tell he was serious.

"What are you thinking about?" I asked flipping the question on him. He was still buried deep inside of me so I tried to accept as much as I could, but even on soft his dick was still a menace to society.

It took him a little while to spit it out, but I stayed patient because I saw that he was getting a little choked up.

"I can't believe I finally got you," he said sincerely as I finally lifted myself off of him. I wanted to be able to reach his forehead so that I could plant a big kiss there.

"Ay remember when you asked me what my new dreams had been about earlier?" I nodded because he had evaded the question so well.

"They're about you, Tatum. See I've been putting a lot of shit in perspective lately. Like yeah I got a nice house now, but it ain't really a home if it's just me here, right? And I've had plenty of sex, but after a while that shit feels empty when it's not your soulmate," he said sounding more mature than I'd ever heard him be before.

"And last but not least I've got all of this fame and good fortune, but it doesn't mean anything without a family," he said before holding eye contact with me. "I know you won't be moving in with me right now, but I got this house in particular because I believe in you. You're already a staple at ESPN so it only makes sense that you should live near Bristol. Or rather *we* should live near Bristol because this is it for me, Rogers. And eventually I'm gonna want to call you Mitchell if you catch my drift."

I was rarely rendered speechless especially in a conversation with an athlete, but when the words finally came to mind all I could do was smile.

"You really like me, don't you?" I beamed, but he just gestured around him at all he had gone through to get me here.

"What do you think?"

"So why didn't you just say something instead of being so damn aggy all this time?"

"Nah I wasn't about to let you do me like you do them other niggas, Teflon Tatum," he said sarcastically and I couldn't help but laugh at the old nickname I'd gotten at Rutgers from the guys who claimed I never let anything they said or did stick to me.

"Oh, but blowing a big bag on me was so much better and discrete, right? And you better have a nice nest egg put up for retirement because I don't fuck broke men like this."

"Guess it's a good thing I got you out of the way now then since I might not be able to afford you in three years," he joked before I pinched him.

"Nah you know me. I've gotten a bag, lost a bag, then got

another, but I'm never gonna be broke again," he said definitively.

"Oh trust me I know. I'm still surprised you bought this house because everybody knows how cheap you can be."

"Did you ever think that I was just saving up for you?" he asked and I rolled my eyes because now he was just doing too much but in a good way. "And whoever said I was cheap was just hating anyway."

"Who said it was just one person? Don't even try it, Beau. You know you used to have tongues wagging about your on and off the field activities."

"Yeah well the only wagging tongue you need to be worrying about now is mine when it's between your legs every night," he said so casually that I didn't even realize what he meant until he started rubbing my ass.

"Hey I thought I told you nothing was going near my butt today."

"What about this?" he asked as he darted out his tongue in a nasty way.

"Ew is that what you were doing down there?" I asked playfully, but I knew that I was about to make another exception to my rules.

"But wait before you get riled up again. I have to tell you something." I guess my voice sounded pretty serious because he immediately sat up then gave me his undivided attention.

"You were right before when you said that I don't always speak my mind on my show. And the truth is that I did believe you would win the game, but I didn't want to go against what everybody else was saying."

"So if you thought I would win, then why didn't you bet that way?"

"I did. In fact I bet every dollar I had to my name on you. The only reason I lost was because y'all only won by two points so you didn't cover the spread. I had you up by at least fourteen, champ," I told him honestly as I kissed his forehead again.

"Damn hearing you call me that feels so good," he moaned out. "You want to spinnanight with me and say it again and again?" he asked trying to sound like a kid.

I smiled then assured him that I was for sure staying because I was not getting back on that damn helicopter for anything in the world tonight. Plus I had lost count of how many times we'd made each other come so I figured we might need to go into overtime to find out who the real champ was.

FOLLOW ME

Thanks for reading! If you don't want to miss out on any updates about future works of mine then find me on all social media platforms as TanSaidWhat, sign up for my mailing list, and join my reading group Turning The Page With Tanzania Glover.

Visit www.tanzaniaglover.com

And if the cover art took your breath away as much as it did mine, check out the talented artist New Levels Graphics! Thank you so much for bringing this couple to life!

THANK YOUS

I said that I was done writing dissertations to my family and friends in this section so I'll try to keep this brief especially since my love for them has remained the same since the first time I did this. But I do want to say that I feel like the luckiest person in the world to be able to go on this journey with people who genuinely love and care for me. Because of the immense amount of love and support that I receive from them, I get to do the thing I love most in the world and I'm forever grateful for it.